This book is dedicated to my family,
and especially my parents who taught us that sharing is best.

JANETTA OTTER-BARRY BOOKS

That's Mine! Copyright © Frances Lincoln 2010
Text and illustrations copyright © Jennifer Northway 2010

First published in Great Britain in 2010 and in the USA in 2011
by Frances Lincoln Children's Books, 4 Torriano Mews,
Torriano Avenue, London NW5 2RZ

www.franceslincoln.com

British Library Cataloguing in Publication Data
available on request

ISBN 978-1-84780-215-6
Illustrated with watercolour

Printed in Heshan, Guangdong, China by Leo Paper Products Ltd. in July 2010

1 3 5 7 9 8 6 4 2

That's Mine!

Jennifer Northway

FRANCES LINCOLN
CHILDREN'S BOOKS

William and his friend David were playing in the park.

"Watch me, Mom!" called William.

"I'm watching you, William," called Mom, but she wasn't... she was having to sort out Emma, *again*!

"You're always paying attention to Emma,"
complained William on the way home. But Mom
didn't hear, because Emma was crying too loudly.

"Can David come and play with me now?" asked William.

"Maybe tomorrow," said Mom. "I need to get Emma cleaned up."

"Emma spoils everything," complained William. "I'm tired of having a little sister! Can't she go somewhere else?"

"No, she can't go anywhere else!" laughed Mom.
"Here's where she belongs, just like you do."

But William was fed up with Emma. At supper, he didn't
want to sit on his new big chair any more. He wanted to sit
in his old high chair. But Emma was in it!

"This is *my* high chair, isn't it, Mom?" asked William.

"Yes, it *was*," agreed Mom, "but you're much too big for it now."

"Why don't you feed me any more like you're feeding Emma?" asked William.

"Because a big boy like you can feed yourself now!" laughed Mom.

At bathtime Emma's favorite toy was
always William's boat.

"It's my boat really, isn't it?" asked William.

"Of course it is, William," agreed Mom.

"And it's very nice of you to share your toys with Emma."

At bedtime Emma wanted
William's Spotty Cat!

"No! " shouted William.
"I won't share Spotty Cat!"

He was tired of sharing Mom
and everything else with Emma,
and Spotty Cat was his favorite toy.

Next day, William didn't want to go to playschool.
  "I want to stay at home with you, like Emma does,"
he said to Mom.

"That would be nice," said Mom. "But then
you wouldn't get to play with David. He'll be
waiting for you at playschool."

"I used to stay with you all day," said William sadly.
" And now Emma does! Are you sure she can't go
somewhere else? Maybe someone else can have her."

"No," said Mom, hugging William.
"She's here to stay. Just like you."

After playschool William went round to
David's house. But they couldn't play a good game,
because David's little brother wanted all the toys!

David's mom told them all to play nicely together.
"But Mom, he's taking my toys!" wailed David.
"Well, let him have the ones he wants," said David's mom.
"You know you should share toys."

"He only wants them because I'm playing with them," complained David. "And he always cries and gets me into trouble if I don't give them to him!"

"Just like Emma!" said William. "But I never give her Spotty Cat – he's mine, and she can't have him!"

Emma looked poorly when William came
home from David's house. She cried and cried
all afternoon. By bedtime, she would only stop
being cross and miserable if William hugged her.

"Why won't she stop crying?" asked William.

"Her gums hurt because she's getting a new tooth," said Mom. "You used to cry when your teeth hurt. Do you remember?"

"I never cried," said William, "because I had Spotty Cat!"

He thought for a while.

"Do you think if I lent Emma Spotty Cat she might stop crying?"

"Well, it *might* help," said Mom, "but it's up to you.
I know Spotty Cat is very special."

"But I'm only going to lend him to her,
just for now," said William.
"Of course," said Mom.

When Emma had her arms round Spotty Cat
she stopped crying and soon went to sleep.

"I didn't *give* Spotty Cat to Emma," William told Mom. "I just *lent* him."

"I know, William," said Mom. "But you've been the best big brother ever – look how quiet and happy she is now!"

Spotty Cat was a bit wet now, and smelled of Emma, but William didn't mind too much – he had a nice warm feeling inside.

"Emma can't help it when she cries," he told Mom. "You just have to know the right way to comfort her."

"You're right there," agreed Mom. "Lucky for us you're so good at it."

"I think we should get Emma a spotty cat of her own,"
said William. "I think she really needs one."

"What a good idea," said Mom.

"Yes," said William. "So it's a good thing Emma's
got me to look after her, because I'm the best
big brother anywhere!"